Wel ome!

Dear Reader,

Welcome to a world of imagination!

My First Story was designed for 5-7 year-olds as an introduction to creative writing and to promote an enjoyment of reading and writing from an early age.

The simple, fun storyboards give even the youngest and most reluctant writers the chance to become interested in literacy by giving them a framework within which to shape their ideas. Pupils could also choose to write without the storyboards, allowing older children to let their creativity flow as much as possible, encouraging the use of imagination and descriptive language.

We believe that seeing their work in print will inspire a love of reading and writing and give these young writers the confidence to develop their skills in the future.

There is nothing like the imagination of children, and this is reflected in the creativity and individuality of the stories in this anthology. I hope you'll enjoy reading their first stories as much as we have.

Jenni Harrison

Editorial Manager

Ima ine. .

Each child was given the beginning of a story and then chose one of five storyboards, using the pictures and their imagination to complete the tale. You can view the storyboards at the end of this book.

There was also the option to create their own story using a blank template.

The egin ing. .

One sunny day, Emma and Ben were walking the dog.

Suddenly, the dog started barking at a magic door hidden in a tree.

They opened the door and it took them to...

... what is on the other side of the door? Tell us your story!

SOUTH EAST ADVENTURES
CONTENTS

Winner:

Yahya Abubakar (7) - St Paul's   1
Way Foundation School, London

Clifton Lodge School, Ealing

Aiden Pattani (6)   3

Drapers' Maylands Primary School, Harold Hill

Amber Rose Robinson (6)   4
Daisy Edith Sadiku (7)   5
Emaddin Elkish (6)   6
Kacie-Leigh Sue Cooper (6)   7
Alexandra Victoria Parylak (6)   8
Jiya Popat (5)   9

Independent Jewish School, Hendon

Millie Glass (7)   10
Adina King (7)   12
Libby   14
Zaki L   16
Gabi Peston (7)   18
Racheli Laitner   20
Noam Moss (7)   22
Orly Hamburger (7)   23
Danya Friedmann (8)   24
Shayna B   26
Eitan Kaye (7)   27
Shani Bolsom   28
Danielle Speigel (7)   30
Aharon Gabay (7)   31
Joshy Levy   32
Rachel Sinclair   33

Liora Schischa   34
Eitan Aharonovich (8)   35
Jamie Herman (7)   36
Aviv   37
Amelie G   38
Netanel Citron   39
Rinat   40

Melcombe Primary School, Hammersmith

Alyssa Kelly (6)   41
Lujain Abdelrahman   42
Abdelkarim (6)
Annalise Kelly (6)   44
Nour Oussama El Abed (6)   45
Amira Mohamed Iman (6)   46
Nayan Iftikhar (6)   47
Bernardo Sampaio Cerda   48
Florencio (6)
Máté Dinnyési (6)   49
Alliah Arias (6)   50
Charlie Leech (6)   51
Diana Namazova (6)   52

Milton Park Infant School, Southsea

Kieran Rollinson (7)   53
Ellis Paterson   54
Lily Valentine (7)   56
Layan Abdullah Almuneef (7)   57
Lena Rasinska (7)   58
Tommy Bishop (7)   59
Isabelle Kilburn (7)   60
Tyler James Holmes (6)   61
Rosie Tyler (7)   62
Calsy Siddall-Young (7)   63

Alfie Valentine (6)	64	Ivan Qiam (6)	97
Charlie Morgan (6)	65	Gwilym Harris (6)	98
Casey Kathleen Simpson (7)	66	Edith May Fisher (6)	99
Katie Mathis (6)	67	Milly McNicol (6)	100
Brooke Fyfield (6)	68	Honey Lemmon (6)	101
Blake Newman (7)	69	Lydia Stockel (6)	102
Jake Longley (7)	70	Yolo Gunnar Woodman (6)	103
Karolina Rocha Leite (6)	71	Lenny Lovesey (6)	104

Peter Hills CE Primary School, London

George Wadsworth (6) — 105
Ryan Terry Goodier (6) — 106
Bella Soper (6) — 107
Oliver O'Connell (6) — 108

Kayla Ximines-Cummings (7)	72
Maisie Smith (7)	74
Henry Thomas Dean McAleer (7)	75
Arya Parwany (7)	76

Alia Cheverton (6) — 109
Lucas Taylor (6) — 110
Lorelai Vincent (6) — 111
Macy Mead (6) — 112
Poppy Ryan (6) — 113

Shaftesbury Park Primary School, Battersea

Arthur Imankerdjo-Lambert (7)	77
Naomi Knutell (7)	78

St Paul's Way Foundation School, London

Israa Tribak (7)	114
Jannah Kolil Uddin (7)	115
Mohammed Shayaan Abdullah (7)	116
Ayah Tribak (7)	117
Jedidiha Dobamo Aleling (8)	118
Blake Liam Michael Power (6)	119
Feliks Szyszka (7)	120
Ava Miah (7)	121
Zoharin Choudhury Tabassum (7)	122
Jibrael Abdur-Rahman (7)	123
Olivia Karamac (6)	124

Soho Parish CE Primary School, London

Tacita Snape Holmes (7)	79
Eleanor Berenice Kinn (8)	80
Zaakir Abdourahman Ateye (7)	83
Mansura Ali Haioty (7)	84
Lea Rose Aknin (7)	85

St Luke's Primary School, Brighton

Bonnie Bluebelle Lawrence (6)	86
Olivia Marsden (6)	87
Sophie Ridsdale (6)	88
Sylvie Eliza King (6)	89
Jesse Hogan (6)	90
Alice Hogan (6)	91
Maxwell Robinson (6)	92
Echo Capaldi (6)	93
Jonah Peter Driver (6)	94
Noa McQue-Moore (6)	95
Florrie Rees-Francis (6)	96

St Swithun Wells Catholic Primary School, Chandlers Ford

Florence Osman (6)	125
Michelle Appiah (6)	126
Grace Amelia Rayner (6)	127

Whitehall Park School, Islington

Lola Sophia Uppal	128
Watkinson (7)	
Rosie Simmons (6)	130
Clemy Katz (6)	132
Gabriel Baden (7)	134
Anouk Lola Archet-Elsley (6)	135
Helen Kim Wood (7)	136
Alisa Makarova (6)	137
Izzy Potton	138
Genevieve Outten (6)	139

The Stories

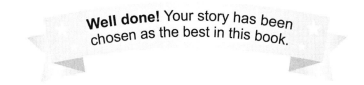

Well done! Your story has been chosen as the best in this book.

Seewid And Wizard Enter A Spooky Forest

Once upon a time, there was a little boy named Seewid who loved discovering new things. One day, he found a wizard watching him. He went to the wizard and the wizard put a spell on the little boy. The spell taught him invisibility and the wizard took him to a magic door.

When they went into the magic door, the door disappeared. The wizard and the boy found themselves dropping from the sky and landed on a path. As they slowly stood up they tiptoed down the path and there stood a horrible witch. She threw Seewid and the wizard into a spooky forest with very long grass. The boy and the wizard found a map. They started walking forward and found eight graves and a red button. They pressed the red button and lots of skeletons came out of the graves. The skeletons were called Freddies.

They started chasing after the wizard and the boy. The witch was controlling the Freddies with an iPad.

The wizard and the boy finally found another door and they went into it, it took them back home. The wizard disappeared and the boy no longer had invisibility powers.

Yahya Abubakar (7)
St Paul's Way Foundation School, London

The Found Treasure

... a desert in ancient Egypt. When the dog and I stepped inside, the dog could talk! 'Where are we?' asked the dog.

'We are in the desert in what looks like ancient Egypt. Look at the pyramids over there,' I replied, pointing in the distance.

'Let's go and explore,' said my dog.

We went to the pyramid and walked inside. It was very dark but some torches lit up the passageway. We got to the middle and found a big room full of shiny treasure, but it was guarded by an ugly monster with sharp teeth and big claws. Luckily for us, he was asleep. I looked at my dog and said, 'Let's get some treasure to take back with us.' I filled my backpack, then I heard the monster waking up. 'Run!' I cried. Me and my dog ran as fast as we could back to the door we got here from. The monster was behind us, but we made it out just in time.

Aiden Pattani (6)
Clifton Lodge School, Ealing

The Island

Once upon a time, Ben and Emma were walking their dog. The dog was barking at a magic door. They walked in and saw a magical treasure chest. The treasure was magnificent, but Ben was amazed when he saw a big pirate ship. The angry pirate said, 'Hey! Who's touching my treasure?'
'But we found it first.'
'Well, you are going to walk the plank!'
They were scared but they went in the water with a splash. Then, two dolphins were under the water. Ben said, 'Hooray!' because dolphins swam them to safety. They decided they would never ever go into the door again.

Amber Rose Robinson (6)
Drapers' Maylands Primary School, Harold Hill

The Island

When they opened the door, they saw a wooden boat, then they got on it. They saw an island. Then they saw some treasure in a sparkly treasure box. Ben spotted a pirate boat, it was gigantic. But then a pirate came to the super island and he said, 'Get away from my treasure!'

'But we found it first!' said Ben and Emma.

Then the angry pirate said, 'Walk the plank!'

Emma was very scared and Ben was too. Out of the sea swam two brilliant dolphins and they saved Ben and Emma. They thought they would never go in the door again and they were happy.

Daisy Edith Sadiku (7)

Drapers' Maylands Primary School, Harold Hill

Behind The Door

Behind the door, Ben and Emma found a boat and they set off on the shimmering blue sea. They chatted while sailing. Next, Ben and Emma found an island. On the beautiful island, they were amazingly happy. Then a furious pirate said, 'Get away from my treasure!' They were really scared. The pirate had a peg leg and looked quite scary. Then the furious pirate said, 'Walk the plank!' They thought they would drown but then some shiny dolphins swam them home. They were fantastically surprised. Then Ben and Emma ran to their beautiful, lovely home.

Emaddin Elkish (6)
Drapers' Maylands Primary School, Harold Hill

My First Story

Ben and Emma found a door. Behind the door there was a brown boat. They sailed for days until they reached an odd island. When they reached the island, they could see a brown treasure chest. In the distance, they saw a ship coming towards them. On the ship was an old, ugly and smelly pirate. He said, 'Give me all your treasure, otherwise you will walk the plank.'
When they walked the plank, two dolphins caught them. After that, they took Ben and Emma home. After, they never went into the door again.

Kacie-Leigh Sue Cooper (6)
Drapers' Maylands Primary School, Harold Hill

The Magic Door

The children and the dog sailed on the boat. The children found a treasure chest but a pirate snatched the treasure chest from the children. The boy ran off the boat and he was very scared. The children jumped on some dolphins and they swam very fast. The children then wore pirate clothes because they went on a super fun adventure.

Alexandra Victoria Parylak (6)

Drapers' Maylands Primary School, Harold Hill

Emma And Ben's Treasure

They got on the boat. Emma stood on the treasure chest and Ben saw a pirate boat.
The pirate said, 'Oi, that is my treasure!'
Emma and Ben ran and they would never come back to the magic door.

Jiya Popat (5)

Drapers' Maylands Primary School, Harold Hill

Losing The Jewel Of Pets

In Downtown, the sunniest town in the world, there was a park. I have two pets, Zoe (a dog) and Penny Ling (a panda) who I always took to the park. One day, we were walking when I suddenly noticed a door. I asked someone, 'Do you know what this door is?' They just shrugged. I turned to the door and asked my pets, 'What is this door?' Do you know?'

Zoe is a dog, a furry golden retriever. Penny Ling is a panda who has black fur and a white patch over her right eye. I have a sparkly, lovely, pretty gem that means I can understand them. They both said at once, 'No.'

I was starting to wonder what this door was and where it led. It made me very puzzled. I was determined to find out. I crept closer and closer.

I couldn't find my jewel. I had it five minutes ago. I could not possibly have lost it now, not at this moment! I was in the worst position to lose it! The jewel meant the world to me. I was about to cry. Penny Ling started to talk. I thought she was saying to open the brown door. So I opened the door and we stepped inside...

We all spun until we hit the floor of a jungle. We looked around and found a map. It looked ancient so I carefully unravelled it to see a riddle that said 'Follow the map. If you do it wrong there will be no luck'. I was puzzled at first but suddenly, I worked it out. It meant follow the path for two minutes, then turn the map upside down and it will reveal the way to find the jewel. I found it!

We went home to find everyone lounging about on the sofa. I told them about my amazing adventure, but they didn't believe me. They're just happy that we have the jewel back. I went to bed and wrote a note. They read it in the morning.

Millie Glass (7)
Independent Jewish School, Hendon

The Space Adventure

I woke up in a flash, bursting with excitement. Today was the day, it was finally my birthday party! We had just had a big slice of cake each when Leah and I decided to explore my neighbour's garden through a hole in the fence. Leah has brown, curly hair and is braver than anyone else I have ever known. We took my dog who was very cute and little. We walked up to an enormous tree and suddenly I noticed a door hidden beneath the branches. Leah persuaded me to go in with her.

Eventually, we opened the magical door. Suddenly, we dropped down a hole and ended up in outer space! We saw some aliens. They made suits for us and even made one for Alfy the dog. They took us in a spaceship that the captain alien was driving. He drove everyone to the moon, Mars, then finally, Uranus.

'What an adventure!' I cried. Although I had a really fun time, I felt scared and worried that I would never get home. We got out of the alien ship and suddenly, one of the aliens spotted a tree with a magic door.

'Look, it's just like how we came to space!' cried Leah.

Finally, I opened the door. This time we didn't fall into a hole, but instead we saw an alien in the tree. He asked us where we wanted to go and offered us a lift home. Eventually, we made it back just in time for my birthday party.

'Where were you?' everyone cried. 'We've been looking for you everywhere!'

'It's a long story,' I muttered, looking at Leah and giggling.

Adina King (7)
Independent Jewish School, Hendon

The Magic Door

A long time ago, Libby's father built her a huge green tree house as a birthday gift. Noah, Marlow and Libby were playing in the tree house when they noticed a mystery door. In excitement, Libby was determined to open the door. The three of them gasped in shock at what they saw...
Noah, Marlow and Libby stepped into Sweety Land!
'I knew that was not a good idea. Let's go home,' said Noah. They turned around and the door had disappeared. They carried on walking and they met a talking tree.
'Hello,' Libby said nervously.
'Hello,' said the tree.
'Can you tell us how to get home?' asked Libby.
However, the talking tree was silent.
'Fine then, evil tree,' said Noah.
Noah, Marlow and Libby carried on walking slowly and then they met a multicoloured talking lollipop.
'Hello lollipop, can you tell us how to get home?'
Finally, the lollipop helped them. She directed them back to the magical door they came through and at last, they got out. They were back in the tree house.

14

Libby looked at her watch and gasped. She realised it was Mum and Dad's wedding anniversary and they had to get home in time for the party. They raced home and made it back just in time. What an adventure they had been on!

Libby

Independent Jewish School, Hendon

The Space Dream

One sunny day, Racheli was filling her rocket up with petrol in preparation for our adventure in space. Racheli had long hair and blue eyes. I was older than her, but she was taller. The rocket was blue like blueberries and as fast as lightning. Finally she finished and we were ready to take off on our adventure.

As we were almost at our first stop on Mars, the rocket started running out of petrol. We started to fall back down to Earth. I cried to Racheli, 'You didn't put enough petrol in the rocket, we are still plummeting to Earth!'

We were hoping we would make it to another planet. I screamed and ran quickly to the window and looked out. 'Aaahhh!' I screamed. We were crashing. At that moment I thought I would never see my mum and dad ever again. Alfi ran as fast as he could. He pulled the rocket along in space as fast as he could. We glided along to Jupiter without falling down like a shooting star. We were all extremely happy because we thought we would never see our family again. I said to Alfi, 'Well done, Alfi!' and gave him a biscuit.

Suddenly, I woke up with a start. I realised it was just a dream and I had fallen out of bed! I went downstairs and told my family about my amazing adventure.

Zaki L

Independent Jewish School, Hendon

Lightning, Merlok And Me

One sunny day, I was walking in the park when suddenly, I noticed a magic door in a huge tree. My mum let me go to the park alone but told me not to go off the path. I didn't listen. I went into the deepest forest and I couldn't resist entering the door. I was usually scared but today I was feeling braver than I had ever felt. I turned the handle and fell into the middle of outer space!

I kept falling through space at the speed of light. I thought I would never stop falling. *Where will I land?* I thought to myself. Suddenly, I landed on the moon. I saw a wizard and a dog. I thought I would never get home. I asked the wizard his name. He was called Merlok and his dog was called Lightning. He was so fast and had blue and white stripes on his fur.

Merlok appeared behind me. 'How did you do that? It's incredible!' I shrieked.

'It takes a lot of practice,' said Merlok.

Merlok finally offered to teach me. It took five hours until I finally got it right. I was focused and trying to remember everything Merlok taught me, when suddenly, I appeared in front of the magic door! Just then, my mum was right beside me.

I was so relieved that my mum was with me and I was finally home!

Gabi Peston (7)

Independent Jewish School, Hendon

The Scary Sandy Adventure

One glorious day, I was walking my dog Oscar. Oscar was a cheerful and brave dog and loved adventures. Suddenly, I noticed a door in a tree. We entered the magic door and felt tingles all through our bodies. A few seconds later, we stepped out and entered a shimmering forest. A trail of dust was on the ground, so we decided to follow it. It led to the heart of the forest. As we continued further in, Olivia asked me frantically, 'When can we go home?'

'First we must get to the end of the trail,' I replied, determined to see what was in store. Suddenly, we heard a noise. It was a scream coming from a witch. She came and cast a spell on me. I fainted. Olivia stared at me thoughtfully. She was about to leave me and go home with Oscar, but as she went to take a step away, something popped into her head. A snake was in the trees and Olivia screamed at the top of her voice. The snake heard, so it swung down and pounced straight at me. I knew it was poisonous. It bit me and I came back to life. We got a tingle and it meant it was time to go home.

A few seconds later, a taxi arrived to take us back to the tree. We stepped out and in a split second, we were back on the beach road.

Racheli Laitner
Independent Jewish School, Hendon

Noam's Space Adventure

One sunny afternoon, I was at the park. I suddenly remembered the tree house I had made with my dad when I was five at the edge of the woods. I dashed off to see if it was still there. Instead, I saw a door on the side of the tree. My tree house had disappeared. *What could have happened to it?* I thought to myself. However, I had to see what was on the other side of this door. I stumbled inside and fell into the darkness of space.

I landed on the moon with a thud and saw a pond. Suddenly, I stumbled into a hole. 'Ouch!' I cried as a rabbit bit me. Quickly, I thought of something. I dashed into the pond so I could hide, but I quickly realised there were crocodiles in the murky water. *Now what?* I thought, before hiding in a bunch of nettles. I looked behind me and saw the rabbit.

'Sorry,' he said sadly. 'I'm Bobby and I'm a wizard.' He waved his wand and I was in a rocket.

'Take me home,' I said. I sat down at the beds I saw in the corner when suddenly, I fell out, deep into space. I landed on a hard carpet with a bump. When I opened my eyes, it was just a dream.

Noam Moss (7)

Independent Jewish School, Hendon

The Deep Blue Sea

One sunny day, my dog Bob and I were on our way to the seaside. It would be Bob's first time swimming in the sea. I could hear him squealing with excitement as we finally arrived. We were going to the seaside because we wanted to go for a swim in the sea. Bob was a brown, fluffy dog who loved going on adventures.

We finally arrived at the seaside and all dove straight in. Suddenly, in the distance we saw something coming towards us. We swam closer and closer and soon saw what it was. There were terrifying sharks coming towards us as fast as a zooming rocket! I was so frightened, but Bob carried on swimming and didn't notice the sharks. A shark swam right up to us and was about to eat us! It had terrifyingly sharp teeth, blue scales all over and loved eating tuna fish. Bob kicked the shark with his foot. The shark flew up into the air and landed all the way where his family were. Bob had not noticed what had happened. The shark was so frightened that he never came back again! Eventually, we made it home. We learned that we must always look out for strangers wherever we are, even if they are animals!

Orly Hamburger (7)
Independent Jewish School, Hendon

Adventure To The Beach

One sunny day, my brother James and I took my new dog, Alfy, to the beach. We had just got Alfy and this was his first time at the beach. Alfy was small and bouncy with white, fluffy fur. He was howling with excitement as we got closer to the seaside. As soon as we stepped onto the beach, Alfy dove straight into the sea.

We were splashing in the sea, but eventually James and I had had enough. We got out and left Alfy splashing around. However, as he was having so much fun, he started floating further and further out until we could barely see him anymore.

James found a magic door which had a lasso sticking out of it. James ran at the speed of lightning to go back and rescue Alfy. We could see him struggling and panicking in the distance. *Would he ever trust us again?* we thought to ourselves. James swung the lasso over Alfy's head and pulled him back to shore. Alfy was wagging his tail because he was so happy that we had rescued him.

Finally, we got home and celebrated by having a disco party with all our friends. We promised Mummy that we wouldn't take Alfy anywhere else ever again.

Danya Friedmann (8)

Independent Jewish School, Hendon

The Scary Spooky Forest

One sunny, hot day, I went to the park. I was on my own. I went to pick pretty flowers for my friend for her birthday. Suddenly, I saw a door in a tree. I was feeling brave so I put down my flowers and pushed open the door. Immediately, I fell into a hole and ended up in a scary, spooky forest.

I saw a witch and a wizard dressed up in pointy hats and black cloaks with scary, pointed teeth. They were very spooky! The witch and the wizard were making the forest more spooky. It was very haunted and terrifying. They were shooting bullets at me. Suddenly, the wizard turned himself into a nice person and he helped me get rid of the witch. He took me to the right place because I knew where we were. We played for a long time. Eventually, we stopped playing games and I helped the wizard collect some potions from the magic woods to get rid of the witch. We stirred the magic potions together and made the witch disappear into thin air.

We walked home together and it was a really long walk. Finally, we got home. We told Mum all about what happened. We all celebrated because the mean, horrible, slimy witch was gone!

Shayna B

Independent Jewish School, Hendon

The Cruel Alien

One sunny day, my dog Bob, Joshy and I were walking in a green, beautiful forest. Joshy was brave and strong and Bob was as long as a sausage dog. Suddenly, Joshy spotted a huge tree that towered over all the other trees in the forest. We walked closer and realised there was a door in this tree. Joshy, being the brave boy he was, opened the magic door and we stepped inside. Immediately, we fell through a hole and ended up in outer space!

I met an alien who chucked us into a massive cage. The alien missed Bob, so Bob wandered around. He ended up on Jupiter and there were thunderstorms and tornados everywhere! Bob felt terrified and suddenly, a tornado tried to catch Bob. He ran off Jupiter as fast as he could. When Bob was off Jupiter, he kept on running. Eventually, Bob spotted an alien guarding his friends in a silver cage. When the alien got bored, he wandered off. Bob bit through the cage and we all escaped.

At last we made it home. I felt so proud of myself for getting away from the cruel alien that trapped us in the cage.

Eitan Kaye (7)
Independent Jewish School, Hendon

The Spooky Forest (An Extract)

It was a beautiful day, so I decided to go to the forest with my dog, Oscar. I was going to the forest because I wanted to experience an adventure with my dog. I went to get some food to eat on our trip, before setting off in the sunshine. As we arrived at the forest, Oscar started howling and something didn't feel right. Oscar was a very lively dog who loved going to the forest.

Oscar tried to show me, but I couldn't understand. He started tugging at his leash and pulled me along, so I followed him. When I followed him, I said, 'Stop! Oh no, I can hear something.'

Suddenly, a witch came out of nowhere. I started running away but the witch followed and put a spell on me. The spell made me go into a deep sleep.

Oscar ran back to the house and thought who he could run to for help. He went to my friend's house to see if she could help. Oscar growled and growled until she finally listened and started to follow him back to the forest.

She rescued me and took me back home to safety. The witch was nowhere to be seen.

Shani Bolsom
Independent Jewish School, Hendon

The Spooky Forest

One stormy day, I was with my dog Oscar. Even though it was pouring with rain, I still had to take him for a walk. I promised my mum I would and I always keep my promises.

I was in the park with beautiful flowers that were as red as poppies. Suddenly, I saw a strange tree that had a door in it. The door was brown with yellow stripes. When I stepped through the door, I arrived at a strange place called The Spooky Forest.

There was a sign pointing to a witch's house. Oscar and I were scared to knock on the witch's door. Oscar and I had to be brave so we could be friends with her. We bravely knocked on the door. The witch opened the door and shrieked, 'Who are you and what is your name?'

I did not answer because she had a green face and purple hair. She looked terrifying. Then I said, 'I just want to go home and be safe again.'

The witch wanted to make a deal with us. She told us she would help us get home if we became her friends. We agreed because we were so gleeful.

Danielle Speigel (7)
Independent Jewish School, Hendon

In The Ocean

One sunny day, I was walking with my brother Zaki in the park. Suddenly, Zaki spotted a door. I opened it carefully and slowly. Out of nowhere, we both landed on a pirate ship...

'Where are we?' said Zaki.

'I don't know,' I replied.

Suddenly, a pirate roared out of nowhere. 'Arrrrr!' screamed the pirate.

'Where's the treasure?' I asked bravely.

'Look,' said Zaki, 'a map!'

Whilst I was distracting the pirate, Zaki went to steal the map.

'Walk the plank!' screamed the pirate.

Just then, a big monster named Gogo splashed out of the sea. The two boys whispered to each other, 'How about we give him his favourite food?'

The pirate jumped off the ship and was never seen again. Whilst the monster was eating his favourite food, slime pizza, Zaki saw the magic door on the poster of the ship.

With that, they were at the park again. They walked and walked until they finally got home.

Aharon Gabay (7)

Independent Jewish School, Hendon

Joshy And Rinat's Spooky Adventure

It was a beautiful day, the sun was shining and there was a clear blue sky. Rinat and I were going to the park. It was a lovely journey but when we got there, we noticed a magical door in a tree. Rinat was quite scared but I opened the door to a swirling hole that sucked us straight in. Rinat had blonde hair and brown eyes. She was my little sister. The door brought us to a spooky forest. We stumbled through the terrifying forest and met a witch who walked over to us slowly. She said, 'I am Witchy Witch.' She took some rope and tied it around us. We all started screaming for help, we thought we would be stuck there forever.

We carried on screaming for help and the witch became furious with us. She went out to get her spell book. Meanwhile, Rinat and I gave our voices a rest. When the witch came back, she said in a normal voice, 'Abracadabra!'

The next thing we knew, we were back in the park! Rinat and I didn't stick around to play, we ran home and told our family all about it.

Joshy Levy
Independent Jewish School, Hendon

A Magical Adventure

One sunny morning, my brother Ben, our dog Balloo and myself were at my friend's party. Suddenly, my friend gave Balloo a balloon. As soon as he touched the balloon, *whoosh!* We were off. 'Where are we?' asked Ben.

There was a secret door in front of us. We couldn't resist opening it. We inched closer to the door and eventually carelessly jumped in. Suddenly, we landed on a train track. 'Ahhhh!' we screamed. At that moment, we were dodging trains and finally realised we were getting closer to a train station. Eventually, we got to the train station and luckily we were all okay. We waited for the right train, then hopped onto it and arrived back at our friend's party just in time. We played party games and sang 'happy birthday'. We had delicious chocolate cake to eat. Ben and I looked at each other and winked, knowing we would always remember our special adventure.

Rachel Sinclair
Independent Jewish School, Hendon

The Spooky Adventure

It was a sunny day when me and my dog Alfie were walking through a forest on our way to my best friend Libby's birthday party. Alfie was a happy, jolly dog and loved bouncing through the forest on our walks.

Suddenly, a witch called Mildred popped up out of nowhere. She had a long nose and very long, wavy hair. Mildred screamed so loudly that I fainted! Alfie yelped and lay down on me. He could tell something wasn't right. The witch had cast a spell on me!

Alfie ran to get help from a nearby village. He brought back a group of people to rescue me.

As they arrived, the spell was wearing off and Mildred had disappeared. I felt so happy that she was gone. Some people took me and Alfie back to my warm house. I promised my mum that I would never go on an adventure like that again. I felt so relieved to be back home with my family. What an adventure it had been!

Liora Schischa
Independent Jewish School, Hendon

Space Adventure

One sunny day, I was walking my dog Alfy in the park with my friend Liora. She was very brave and I was quite afraid of everything. Suddenly, I saw a magic door hiding in a tree. Liora opened the door and fell inside. I followed her in and we ended up in outer space!

We saw a rocket floating in the middle of space. It was empty, so Liora opened the door and we crept inside. I panicked and pressed a button.

Immediately, we flew off! Eventually, we landed on a different planet. *This doesn't look like Earth*, I thought to myself, confused and worried that we would never get home. Luckily, at that moment, Alfy grew bigger and suddenly he had wings!

Liora and I yelled, 'Hooray!' We hopped on Alfy and few back home. Once we got home, Alfy became smaller and smaller until he went back to normal. We felt so happy to be back home.

Eitan Aharonovich (8)
Independent Jewish School, Hendon

The Spooky Monster

One cold day, I was walking in the park when suddenly, I found a door on a tree. I stepped into the door and I fell into a spooky forest. I saw a monster that tried to eat me because I was in his forest. Just as he leaned in to gobble me up, I saw a shimmering sword on the ground by my feet. *I'm going to make it out alive*, I thought to myself, hopefully. I grabbed the sword which was as sharp as sharks' teeth and fought off the monster. I stabbed him in the tummy, so immediately he fell to the ground and died.

As last, I found the door out of the tree. I walked towards the door, opened it and suddenly, I appeared in the park. I walked home and my mum was waiting for me. She asked where I had been all this time. I told her I was on an adventure.

Jamie Herman (7)
Independent Jewish School, Hendon

The Space Adventure

One sunny day, Sam was walking his dog, Mylo. He saw a mysterious door so he opened it and it took him to outer space.

They were floating in space and didn't know how to get back. They were stuck there for a month.

Sam and Mylo got so hungry. Sam said something to himself, that he should have listened to his dad and mum.

Sam suddenly saw a wizard called Abra. 'Mylo, look! There's a wizard in front of us!'

'What do you need?' said the wizard.

'We need to go to London.'

Abra had magical powers and he flew them back to London. Sam, Mylo and Abra arrived at a mystery tree. Sam's friend was having a birthday party. Everyone started singing 'happy birthday'. Sam woke up and it was all a dream.

Aviv

Independent Jewish School, Hendon

A Door In A Tree

One sunny day, when I was eight years old, I loved to explore and decided to go on an adventure. I saw a door in a tree and felt so confident to open it. When I did, surprisingly, I landed in a jungle! A scary witch came up to me and I was shaking with fear. She kindly said, 'Please don't be afraid of me, I will help you to get out of here because there are lots of other wicked witches here.'
The other witches heard her and yelled, 'Go to your room!'
I quickly decided to escape and ran back through the jungle, trembling. I found the door in the tree trunk and ran home as fast as I could. I told my family about my adventure, but they didn't believe me!

Amelie G
Independent Jewish School, Hendon

The Spooky Adventure

One sunny day, I was walking in the park with my friend, Shani. She had brown, silky hair and loved to explore. Suddenly, I noticed a magic door in a tree. I thought it was an ordinary door, so I stopped to see. Shani was begging me not to open it, but I was determined to. 'I really want to open the door. I am so sorry but I have to do it, Shani.' I opened the door and we went down into the spookiest forest ever. Shani and I were extremely scared. As we walked through the forest, it became spookier by the minute. Suddenly, a witch appeared and jumped out at us.

Eventually, we got home. I was so relieved.

Netanel Citron
Independent Jewish School, Hendon

My Story

On a sunny, cloudy day, I went to Eitan's birthday party in the small park. The magician came to the party and did some magic tricks. Then Aviv came with a white, medium, square cake. Suddenly, a cheeky pink monster came to the birthday party. The cheeky pink monster ate all the cake super fast. The children in the party were sad. Eitan's mummy and his sister, Ela, had an idea. They went to the bakery to buy a cake. Eitan's mummy and Ela came to the park with the strawberry cake. All the children sang happy birthday for Eitan and ate the cake.

Rinat
Independent Jewish School, Hendon

The Girl That Went Missing

There was a spooky forest and I walked inside. As I was walking, I saw a little cottage, so I walked to it. When I got to the cottage, a squeaky voice said, 'Come in.' I opened the door and I saw a witch! The witch said I have to have green soup and drink green juice because the witch captured me. I wanted to go home.

One morning, I started to cry because I missed my family and friends. I tried to sneak out but the witch saw me. She got angry. I started to shout for help and a boy heard me. He ran as fast as he could. When he got to the witch's cottage, he kicked the door open and saw the witch sleeping. Then the boy tiptoed upstairs and saw a door. He tried to open the door but he couldn't. He looked around for a key. He knew there was a key but it wasn't in the cottage. He went to the garden to look and found the key. He went back to the cottage and unlocked the door. We ran downstairs but the witch saw us. She said she would lock us both in the room, but she couldn't because the boy still had the key. She went to the basement to look for another set of keys. Me and the boy went back to the magic door safely and got back home.

Alyssa Kelly (6)
Melcombe Primary School, Hammersmith

The Spooky Forest

One sunny day, I was walking my dog Frank in the garden when I noticed a magic door hidden in a tree. I opened the door and it took me to a spooky forest.

I started to walk with Frank in the spooky forest when I heard something say, 'Raba, raba, raba!' Then someone screamed, 'Help, help!' I was frightened, after that I ran. Suddenly, I hit someone. It was my teacher, Miss Mosley. We heard that sound again, 'Raba, raba, raba!'

Me and Miss Mosley were screaming, 'Aahhh!'

I said to Miss Mosley and Frank, 'Run!'

Someone said, 'Don't be scared.'

I wondered who it was. It was a frog. I asked him, 'Can you speak?'

The frog said, 'Yes.'

Then Miss Mosley said, 'We have to go back home.'

I said, 'But we don't know the way to the magic door.'

The frog said, 'Go left then you will find someone to help you.'

Me, Miss Mosley and Frank started walking left. After that, we heard laughing sounds. Frank ran to six colourful flowers who were laughing. They said hello.

I said, 'Hello! Can you speak too?'

'You are in a spooky forest, so we can speak,' the flowers said.

I asked the flowers to help us. The pink flower said, 'Go to the old tree, he can help you.'

Then the flowers told us to go to the right of the lake.

We started walking again to find the old tree. We walked for a long time and we asked all the spooky animals, flowers and trees about the old tree. One of the trees said, 'It's my grandpa and he lives on the hill.'

Frank ran up to the hill so me and Miss Mosley followed him.

Finally we found the old tree. I asked the old tree, 'Please help us to go back to the garden before midnight.'

The old tree said, 'Of course.' I noticed there was a magic door hidden in the old tree. The tree said, 'One, two, three, my magic spell comes free. Go from a spooky forest through a magic door to a garden.'

We went back to a garden. That was a nice adventure we had in the spooky forest.

Lujain Abdelrahman Abdelkarim (6)

Melcombe Primary School, Hammersmith

The Wicked Witch

I was in a spooky forest at night. It was really scary and dark. I could see shadows moving in the moonlight. As I continued to walk through the spooky forest, I saw a cottage. I walked up the path to the front door and a squeaky voice said to come in. When I got in, the door closed behind me and I felt scared. I could see some red eyes looking at me. I thought to myself, *what is that?* It was a witch. I ran up the stairs. When I got to the top, there was a door. I opened the door and saw a wizard trapped. I helped him so he took care of the witch and I helped to defeat her. After that, I ran out of her house and through the magic door.

Annalise Kelly (6)

Melcombe Primary School, Hammersmith

Adventure With Butterfly

One sunny day, I was walking in the park with my family. I noticed a magic door hidden in a tree. I opened the door and it took me on an adventure with beautiful, colourful butterflies.

One of them took me, so we flew up high in the sky. I saw amazing things, like mountains, seas, rivers, my school and houses. It was very nice and I had lots of fun. Then we came back, but we lost the way. I was scared and crying. Suddenly, a nice bird saw us shouting, so he took us to the right way.

Finally, we came back to the park. After that, I played and danced with other butterflies. It was a funny and fantastic day.

Nour Oussama El Abed (6)

Melcombe Primary School, Hammersmith

The Magic Door

Jack and Lily were on a school trip in the forest. They saw a huge tree and behind it was a magic door. They started to explore and saw a witch making a potion. She chased them through her house. After that, the witch locked them in a cage. Also, she gave them lots of sweets to make them fat. While she was making the potion, Jack and Lily were asleep. She carefully put the potion in their mouths but before she did, a kind person came to save them. He also broke the spell.

Amira Mohamed Iman (6)
Melcombe Primary School, Hammersmith

The Play Park

The boy found a play park and went to play in it. When he put his foot on the slide, he saw a monster and was scared. Luckily, there was a wizard that used a spell to make the monster melt. It took forever and ever. The wizard and the boy played together in the park. This time, when the boy stepped on the slide, he fell. When he opened his eyes, he saw a treasure chest with lots of gold in it. They shared it, then the boy took it home to show his parents.

Nayan Iftikhar (6)

Melcombe Primary School, Hammersmith

The Happy, Scared Monster

Once upon a time, there was a happy, scared monster called Micky. He jumped into a book. He was in a spooky forest full of ghosts! He was so scared! Anty, the bad ghost, was chasing Micky around. Jamie, the good ghost, decided to help Micky dig a hole in the ground. Micky jumped into the hole and went back home. He went to sleep in his comfy bed and he lived happily ever after.

Bernardo Sampaio Cerda Florencio (6)
Melcombe Primary School, Hammersmith

A Spooky Forest

One Sunday, the boy went for a walk with his dog into a spooky forest. Suddenly, they noticed a magic door hidden behind the big branches. They couldn't open the door. The boy had an idea about how to open it. The boy had to kick the door, there was a spooky witch. The boy was strong and he kicked the witch to the right. They walked over her and found treasure.

Máté Dinnyési (6)
Melcombe Primary School, Hammersmith

Treasure Path

I went to the park and I saw my teacher and the wizard waiting for me, but then I saw notes on the ground. I picked one up and opened it. It said, 'There is treasure buried somewhere in the park'. Then a storm came but luckily, the wizard had a magic umbrella. I found another note and I opened it. It was a map to the treasure. We walked to the treasure.

Alliah Arias (6)

Melcombe Primary School, Hammersmith

Wizard Vs Monster

Once upon a time, there was an evil monster who lived on Planet Zog. He went to his flying saucer and crashed into Earth. On Earth there was a wizard. The monster began to fight the wizard. The monster made a ghost with his hands. The wizard stopped the ghost. The monster was strong but the wizard killed the monster.

Charlie Leech (6)

Melcombe Primary School, Hammersmith

Fun, Spooky Adventure

I was walking with my dog when I noticed a door. I went in innocently. I came to a spooky, dark forest. My dog and I kept walking until we came to another door. I got in and heard a noise. I went to look, then I saw a witch. She was doing something. It looked like she was making a potion.

Diana Namazova (6)

Melcombe Primary School, Hammersmith

Mystery On The Moon

... outer space. I was in a humongous aircraft at 18:00, at night-time. Suddenly, I saw a gas cylinder flying around. A crazy and friendly wizard appeared in the aircraft and the wizard suddenly disappeared again.

Quickly I got on my pearl spacesuit to have a look at it. Suddenly, as soon as I got out, I got on the sticky moon! I was stuck to it. 'Wait a minute, the moon isn't made of cheese,' said Jimmy.

I turned around and Creeky the witch was behind me. Something was wrong but Jimmy didn't know what. 'How strange this is,' replied Jimmy.

'Yes, yes,' recited the witch, dropping the gas cylinder whilst cackling.

Whilst the witch wasn't looking, I stole her gas cylinder and flew off. When the witch finally stopped daydreaming, she chased us on her broomstick. Whilst flying, the wizard reappeared and cast a spell that went like this: 'Boppety boo,' and the moon changed back to normal. We finally found the bright red button that the witch used and pressed to send us back into the aircraft. The witch smacked her fat face on the glass...

Kieran Rollinson (7)

Milton Park Infant School, Southsea

The Big Park

... a noisy, large play park! Jack went running so quickly, so did Kaitlin. 'What shall we go on?' asked Jack. Jack was on the roundabout and Kaitlin went on the slide. Then we were invited to a party. We were so excited and amazed. What a noisy, loud, giant park it was!

We went back to school and made some beautiful presents and small presents. 'Uh-oh!' Jack got hurt by the scissors, pointy, sharp red ones.

We went to the party, it was a happy, amazing, lovely day. We celebrated with a massive, towering cake. We found dangerous and beautiful bugs! Gigantic bugs! We saw green, brown and towering trees. There was suddenly no food there.

We got back to school and we got sandwiches, crisps, sweets, yoghurts, juice, water, chocolate bars and a cake. Miss Joy packed everything in a huge bag. We jumped on a green huge bus to the large tree. We sat on the bus for 15 minutes. We ate and had a huge play. We saw a ginormous blue and white butterfly.

After that we said goodbye.

'Let's go back to school.'
We got on the bus. We got to the calm, beautiful school. On the bus everyone was being friendly.

Ellis Paterson
Milton Park Infant School, Southsea

A Magical Ocean

... a fragment of warm water! I really wanted to find a whale, but how? Then I swam deeper and deeper with my teacher, Miss Diggens, and I thought I actually did see a whale moving, because of the shape of the shadow. 'Look behind that rock,' I said.

'There's nothing there,' Miss Diggins shouted loudly, but it was actually just her making a shadow puppet like a whale moving!

I did wish we had a submarine. Then I actually saw a blue swishy whale and we chased it for a long time. What a fast whale it was! 'Why is it so cold down here?'

Me and Miss Diggins got stuck, lost, in the middle of nowhere. I saw a fish, 'Heeeeeelp!' I shouted. The fish was actually lazy and didn't want to rescue us. I tried to swim but luckily Miss Diggins had some scissors so she snipped us out. Then the whale tried to spray us. 'Don't spray me you little whale!'

Happily, we found gold, 800 bags full of gold! We were rich. We had a celebration and everyone was dancing and meeting other children, also adults.

Lily Valentine (7)
Milton Park Infant School, Southsea

A Spooky Forest

One sunny day I was walking Bibi the dog. We saw a magic door hidden in a tree. I opened the door, the door took me to the spooky forest. I was sitting on the floor, then Bibi the dog ran away. We saw a spooky haunted house and horrible spiderwebs in a tree.

I went in the house and saw a monster in the house with Bibi! I went in so fast that we found a witch in the house. When the door was open the witch came down the stairs, she was a friendly witch with the friendly monster that had my dog. Then my dog ran away again. I tried to find him, he was stuck in the mud. We all tried to get him out and then the witch had the idea, she was pleased to have a friend so she went back home and bought a book. She said a spell and Bibi the dog came out of nowhere! I asked the witch to take us home, she said yes so she took us home. She was so happy, she did a spell to take us home.

The spooky forest was an adventure! I had so much fun with the witch. I had fun on the beautiful and lovely day.

'We will come here again!'

Layan Abdullah Almuneef (7)
Milton Park Infant School, Southsea

Island Of White

One sunny and windy day, a girl called Lexy was walking her dog, Max. They were walking along the street. Suddenly, they saw a magical, old wooden door. So they walked inside. When they were inside, they ended up on the Island of White. After that, they met a wizard called Mr Blake. Mr Blake was a tall wizard with a long, white, curly beard. Max was a dog who barked a lot, but Lexy was a quiet and kind girl. After walking around, they realised they were on a tiny island. They were confused about where they were. Lexy asked, 'Why are we here?'

They saw something shiny in the sand. They dug until they saw some shiny, blue diamonds. Suddenly, they were under the deep, deep water, but they managed to swim out. Then they noticed a brown and red boat and some golden, sparkly treasure. Soon after, Max and Lexy jumped in the boat and sailed back home. They lived happily ever after.

Lena Rasinska (7)
Milton Park Infant School, Southsea

Outer Space Adventure

... outer space!

My name is Tom, I like that name. The monster was called Blobby. The dog was called Alexander, but he is usually called Alex. We lost the magic door, so we had to use our rockets, but when we tried to find them, they were gone!

'What can we do?' I said. 'I see some rockets in a trail. We could follow the trail.'

We followed and followed until we saw there was a monster carrying our rockets.

'What a scary monster! Don't go over there!' I said to Alex.

Alex ignored me. The monster stopped, I ran over, the dog stopped. Really slowly, the monster said he would not steal our rockets but asked if he could stay where we live or keep some of the rockets. We said, 'Stay where we live.'

We all went back home and lived happily ever after.

Tommy Bishop (7)
Milton Park Infant School, Southsea

Going Into The Jungle

... a noisy jungle. I was excited to go on a noisy adventure in the jungle. I saw giant grey elephants and really slow, wet turtles swimming in the blue water. What an exciting jungle adventure this was! Suddenly, I saw a nasty green witch. I screamed. The witch told me her name, it was Zelena. Then, because she was very wicked, she cast a spell on me that would keep me asleep forever. A giant elephant saw me, he was very upset so he put me on his back.

He killed the witch by standing on her because elephants have enormous feet. Then because her magic was gone, I woke up and the elephant was happy. I hugged the elephant and kissed him goodbye and went onto my boat to set sail back home. Me and the thoughtful elephant would really miss each other. I went back home and had a warm cup of tea.

Isabelle Kilburn (7)
Milton Park Infant School, Southsea

A Space Adventure

One sunny day, I was walking my dog when I noticed a magic door hidden in a tree. I opened the door and it took me to space. There I saw a monster, then a witch and she said, 'Abracadabra!' Then there was an alien! The witch ran away and then bumped into a puppy. The dog, witch and puppy ran but the monster was back on their track, so they went left and he went right. Phew! He was gone for now.

The girl, dog and little puppy went off. Meanwhile, there came a spacecraft. It was the alien once again, but luckily there was a knife floating around so the girl grabbed it and stabbed the alien. He died!

It was time for the dog, puppy and the girl to go back home. They lived happily ever after.

Tyler James Holmes (6)
Milton Park Infant School, Southsea

The Girl Who Tries To Defeat The Witch

One spooky night, there was a horrible, cruel witch. There was a girl called Livy and the witch's name was Evie. Evie was trying to destroy lots of islands, but Livy tried to defeat Evie and stop her from destroying islands. But it wasn't just islands, Evie kept destroying the planet. Livy was being brave but she called her rescue dog. But Duncan wasn't calling back. Evie started to chase her. 'Help me!' cried Livy. Duncan heard and he quickly went to save her.

At night, when both of them went to bed, they couldn't get to sleep because they heard lots of noises.

Rosie Tyler (7)

Milton Park Infant School, Southsea

Disneyland

There was a boy called Callum and a girl called Rozie. Callum and Rozie put their stuff down, then they went off to play. When they were playing, a Disney monster came along and took some of their stuff. Then they got a bit sweaty and a bit worn out, so Callum and Rozie had lunch with their little dog. Callum and Rozie were eating with their dog because the dog was very hungry. Callum and Rozie were thirsty and hungry. They all had some cold, fresh water. Rozie asked Callum if he wanted some chips. They went through the magic door and saw Disneyland. They thought it looked amazing.

Calsy Siddall-Young (7)

Milton Park Infant School, Southsea

Untitled

One sunny morning, I was walking my dog when I noticed a magic door hidden in a tree. I opened the door and it took me to a dark, spooky forest full of scary animals. The food they gave me was horrible. It smelled totally disgusting. It looked so funny. I heard a naughty witch saying, 'Ha ha ha!' She smelled like rotten eggs and blue cheese. The creepy witch saw my baby and put him in a volcano. Luckily, the brave superhero came and flew the baby back home. He flew the baby out of the volcano and we lived happily ever after.

Alfie Valentine (6)
Milton Park Infant School, Southsea

Untitled

One sunny day, I was walking my dog when I noticed a magic door hidden in a tree. I opened the door and it took me to a castle. I saw lots of trees around the castle. I could hear leaves falling. From the corner of my eye I saw a king wearing his crown. Then the king asked a knight, 'Can you lift up my shiny throne so I can have a good view?' He tripped up and the king's crown fell off. Then a monster came and ate it! So the knight killed the monster. Afterwards, the king and the knight lived happily ever after.

Charlie Morgan (6)

Milton Park Infant School, Southsea

A Photo For Mum

Once, I saw a sparkly door and I went in it. The door took me to… Africa. I was sleeping and now it was morning. Buster woke up and ran off. A pack of lions appeared. *Roooar!* I ran away. I climbed a hill but I could not see any lion cubs.

'Mrs Smith, what are you doing here?'

'I went after the lion cubs.'

'But there are no lion cubs.'

I had an idea, I had a lion cub costume. I put the costume on Buster and I took the photo home and said, 'Happy birthday Mummy.'

Casey Kathleen Simpson (7)

Milton Park Infant School, Southsea

Untitled

... under the sea. I saw curly coral and I saw a monster with a golden horn. I also saw a dolphin and a mermaid. I could hear octopuses juggling and a whale making music. Then, in front of me, I saw a mermaid princess. She was beautiful. The scary sea monster was hiding behind the rock and he grabbed the mermaid princess with his slimy tentacles. He took her to his cave. The octopus guards swam to the cave. The sea monster tried to eat the mermaid but the sea king came and saved her. They lived happily ever after.

Katie Mathis (6)

Milton Park Infant School, Southsea

The Sea

I went to the sea and then went to the bottom. It smelled like salt. I saw a ship so I swam to it. I had a look inside. I found a chest and I opened it. The chest had treasure in it. It was a bottle of rum. I took it out and and sea snake came to me. The problem was that monsters were after the sparkly chest! Then I saw a sparkly sword at the top of the sea, so I went to get it, then swam back to the ship. I sliced the monster into quarters! I lived happily ever after.

Brooke Fyfield (6)
Milton Park Infant School, Southsea

Final Fantasy XIVV

... Final Fantasy. I met a friendly dinosaur. He was blue and called Yoshi.

'Can you tell me where the pool is, please?' said Bart.

'Go left.'

'OK, bye.' With that, Yoshi jumped in the pool.

They went to the spa, then the pirate zone, then went to bed.

Two weeks later, they met a monster called Godzilla and they became friends.

So the three friends, Bart, Godzilla and Yoshi had another adventure...

Blake Newman (7)

Milton Park Infant School, Southsea

The Spooky Adventure

Once upon a time, a boy was walking his dog in a forest, when the dog fell in a magical hole and a ghost caught him. It took him to its palace to be its pet for a year or so. It kept him in a cage. The others helped him and he ran to his dirty room and went to sleep. The others watched TV, then fell asleep quickly because the black witch turned bad, but then died.

Jake Longley (7)
Milton Park Infant School, Southsea

Finding Treasure

... a play park. As I was walking to the play park, my dog was sniffing around. He found a treasure chest. Then a wizard stole the treasure chest. My dog chased the wizard and he dropped the chest. We had the treasure chest all to ourselves and were rich!

Karolina Rocha Leite (6)

Milton Park Infant School, Southsea

The Epic Space Adventure

Rocksy the dog was walking with her owners, Lilly and Jack. Suddenly, they found a sparkly door. *Poof!* went the door. Lilly and Jack screamed. They opened their eyes and were in space. It was a witch, as nasty as can be. 'Woof! Woof!' went Rocksy.

'We need to take the magic gem, but how?' said Lilly.

'We need to destroy her,' said Jack.

'Lilly, Jack,' said the witch, 'you've made it.'

'Give us the secret gem of power, now!' shouted Lilly. Rocksy started barking at the witch, 'Woof! Woof! Woof!'

'You need to beat my monsters first and whoever gets the most points will win,' said the nasty witch.

'Let's go! Wait, you need a weapon, here you go,' said Lilly. 'Watch out, Jack,' said Lilly. When Rocksy saw that they were losing, she jumped and scratched all the monsters and won.

'Yeah! Well done Rocksy!' said Lilly and Jack.

'Ha ha ha, I tricked you!' said the nasty witch.

'Are you disrespecting me?' said Jack.

'Yes,' said the nasty witch.

Whilst the witch, Lilly and Jack started fighting again, Rocksy stole the secret gem of power and gave it to Lilly.

The gem started to glow, as they ran towards the light that was coming from the open sparkly door.

The door slowly began to close and they got closer.

'Hurry Lilly!' cried Jack.

They jumped through the door as it was about to close, and fell onto the side walk.

'That was an epic adventure,' said Jack.

Lilly sighed and said, 'Let's go home, Mum must be worried.'

'Woof! Woof!' barked Rocksy.

Kayla Ximines-Cummings (7)

Peter Hills CE Primary School, London

The Magic Adventure!

In the forest where he found his family, they all ran and hugged each other tightly. Charlie then invited everyone on an adventure. Just at that moment, a horrible, horrible witch appeared. Charlie's mum grabbed her bag and took out her powerful cube. Everyone was amazed at what that powerful cube could do! Then Charlie's dad told everyone to run all the way to the other side of the forest, but they couldn't get anywhere. The witch mostly wanted the children.

Harry, Charlie's dad, shouted, 'Catch this powerful cube!'

The witch was really loud, so no one could hear a thing. The witch snatched the cube out of Lucy's hand with her magic powers, then she zapped everyone except Charlie. He was hiding behind the tree. He awoke the rest of his family and his friends. They all ran over to where they were before they found the powerful cube, where the witch was lying.

The next day, the witch was lying down. Everyone grabbed her by the arms and legs and they found a cave to put her in. Everyone lived happily ever after.

Maisie Smith (7)
Peter Hills CE Primary School, London

74

Treasure Hunt

In the park, a boy spoke to his friend. His friend said, 'There is treasure in this park.'
'Where is it?' asked the boy nicely.
'I don't know. Someone told me a story about it.'
They thought it would be in sand because treasure is meant to be in sand. Then they looked in some sand and saw treasure! They wondered if there was more. They decided to look in the sandpit and they found more treasure! There was lots of gold. They took the treasure home. Then they went back to the park and saw a dog. He had some treasure and he was alone. They asked if they could keep him. The dog barked 'yes'! They took the dog home.

Henry Thomas Dean McAleer (7)

Peter Hills CE Primary School, London

The Magical Door

In a spooky forest there was a boy, who saw a witch! The boy tried to find the exit but he couldn't! There were lots of bushes in the way, so the boy went to get a stick to chop them down. There was mud all over the ground, so he couldn't run away. At last the boy found the exit and went towards it forgetting about his friend. He went to find him, then the boy had an idea. He had a flashlight in his bag, so he retrieved it and turned it on. It was really dark and there were slimy snails under his feet.

Arya Parwany (7)
Peter Hills CE Primary School, London

The Squid Had Seven Legs

Under the sea, one million years ago, lived a magical ghost pirate and a squid that had only seven legs. The squid was very helpful to others, but was also mocked because of his missing leg. One day, because he was whistling, a ghost pirate appeared. He was so nice and friendly that he asked, 'Hi! How can I help?'

'I need one more leg. Would you give me one?'

'Of course! But first, would you travel across the seven seas with me because I need a friend to find the mighty treasure?'

Then, they both took a marvellous trip across the seven seas. They found the golden treasure and when they opened it, there was a wish inside! In the end, the squid got his mighty leg!

Arthur Imankerdjo-Lambert (7)

Shaftesbury Park Primary School, Battersea

The Witch And The Wizard

Once upon a time in a spooky forest, there was a house. In the house there lived a boy and a girl. Their names were Lily and James.

One day, Lily said, 'Come on, let's go outside!' So they went out.

They kept walking until a shadow appeared on the ground. It was a witch! The witch said, 'I will eat you today!'

Suddenly, a wizard appeared and said, 'I will save you!'

So the witch and the wizard had a battle. The wizard won. Lily and James said, 'Thank you!' They went home and said, 'We will never go out again!'

Naomi Knutell (7)
Shaftesbury Park Primary School, Battersea

Dragon Island

Once, there was a fifteen-year-old girl and she was strolling in the woods when... *bam! Crash!* The woods started to float. 'I'll make a shelter so when it's morning I can set off,' she said. While she was making the shelter, she saw a peculiar rock. She picked it up... it wasn't a rock, it was an egg; not any egg, it was a dragon's egg and through its mind it said, 'Welcome to Dragon Island, and I'm your personal dragon Pingey.' The colours surrounded her. Blue, yellow and red.

After a while the girl could fight and fly with Pingey. She was so good that she was called the Dragon Rider.

In a fight the girl sadly got killed, so the tale is whatever found it will... 'Eeee! Do you think I'm supposed to know, I wasn't there!'

Tacita Snape Holmes (7)

Soho Parish CE Primary School, London

Alice The Explorer

Once, there was a woman called Alice who had a dream that she was to be an explorer.

One day, she woke up and her dog Milo was barking loudly because he had heard a knock on the door. She quickly got her clothes on and opened the door to see a man standing there with a letter in his hand. She took the letter inside and saw that she had won a competition. The prize was that she could go on a boat around the world. It also said that it was on the 1st of July, which happened to be tomorrow. She was so excited that she nearly fell over.

The next day for breakfast, she had a croissant. After that she got on a train. She found a seat, finally, and soon enough the train was going. She waited on the train for 3 hours, then she got off and jumped on another. She got off at Dover, it was a three-minute walk to the boat. She got on the boat and went to France.

She went to the Eiffel Tower in Paris and tried frogs' legs and climbed Mont Blanc and she actually got to the top. Then she got back on her boat and next she went to Spain. In Spain she watched Flamenco dancing. She went to an art gallery and saw paintings painted by Pablo Picasso.

She got on her boat once more and sailed across the Mediterranean Sea to end up in Jordan. She swam in the Dead Sea. After that, she went on a hot-air balloon all the way to Mongolia. In Mongolia she heard a story about the Mongolian Death Worm and drank fermented horse milk. She went back onto her boat and next she went to Australia.

In Australia she met a kangaroo and went scuba-diving in the Great Barrier Reef. Then she sailed to New Zealand and she climbed Mount Cook. She tried Lolly Cake. Then she went to South America, to Brazil, and she saw a jaguar and a scarlet macaw in the Amazon Rainforest. Next she went to Chile and climbed the highest volcano in the world, Ojos Del Salado.

Then she went to Canada and made maple syrup. She climbed Mount Logan then went on to the USA and looked at stories about the Native Americans. By this time Alice was very, very tired so she thought she should go home. She got home fast on a plane and gave her boat away to the people who needed it.

When she got back, Milo her dog jumped and licked her face because he hadn't seen her for so long. He had missed her very much, they both fell asleep in a warm, comfortable bed.

Alice made her dream come true. You can make your dreams come true as well.

Eleanor Berenice Kinn (8)
Soho Parish CE Primary School, London

The Magic Door

Once upon a time there was a dog named Rocket. Rocket found a magic door and it took him to outer space. Rocket saw Ursa Minor, but he wanted to go home. When he tried, the door was gone. Rocket landed on Mars and he met a boy named Jake. 'What happened?'
'I'm lost and I can't find the magic door,' Rocket said. So, they went to find the door together. They went behind the moon. They searched in lots of galaxies. Suddenly, they found the right galaxy. Jake couldn't wait to see Planet Earth. When they saw the door it was sticky, they went inside and Rocket was happy because he found his way home with the help of his new friend, Jake.

Zaakir Abdourahman Ateye (7)
Soho Parish CE Primary School, London

The Forest Of Amazement And Fear

There was a family that lived next to a forest. Mother said, 'Don't go into the nearest forest!' But they did not listen and went in to explore... They got lost!

In the forest they found a funny monster disguise. It was a very useful, long piece of fabric with two eyeholes. Izzy picked it up and managed to wear it with Jake, just in case. They explored the forest, it had so many oak trees. Izzy could see a city in the water, as soon as she bent over they got a fright. They ran away. The moral of the story is listen to your parents, because they know best.

Mansura Ali Haioty (7)
Soho Parish CE Primary School, London

The Treasure Hunt

One sunny day, Laura was swimming in the pool with her friend Sam. They were having lots of fun when he noticed the map next to the pool had disappeared! When they were having fun the pirate came in the house and stole it. Laura and Sam went on a magic boat to the treasure island.

Lea Rose Aknin (7)
Soho Parish CE Primary School, London

The Little Panda

One scorching hot day there lived a little panda who loved to jump. One day she decided to jump to the stars. They were a shiny gold. As she was jumping she fell into a star. 'Ahh!' She fell with a *thud!* She was in a magical forest and she saw chocolate trolls making a river and one-eyed monkeys in the trees. The baby panda saw a creepy castle in front of her. The little panda decided to open the door. There were cobwebs everywhere and a skeleton lion that was actually a camera, and it sent a message to the witch. As the panda was about to escape, the evil witch took her home. She locked her in a dungeon, but she found a magic, giant coconut and it took her back home to the moon.

Bonnie Bluebelle Lawrence (6)
St Luke's Primary School, Brighton

Ella The Mouse

One roasting morning, a mouse called Ella was at a party. She saw a door and decided to go and look at it. It seemed to be leading to a jungle, so she opened the mysterious door and went through. When she felt a *bang!* she knew she had arrived. She broke open the door and saw the jungle. There was a squirrel and a strawberry bush, but when she turned around... she saw an angry tree. He said, 'Why are you destroying my world?'

'I'm sorry,' said Ella.

Just then, Ella remembered that at the party she tickled her friend. So she decided to tickle the tree. Sneakily, she crept up and tickled him so hard that he said. 'Stop! I'll be your friend!'

'OK,' said Ella.

Olivia Marsden (6)
St Luke's Primary School, Brighton

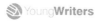

The Twin Apple Tree Fairies

Once upon a time there were twin fairies. One day they were collecting apples and saw a door, so they decided to go through it. When they got to the end the twins saw an apple tree and beautiful flowers. The twins picked loads of flowers and apples, they heard a rumbling sound and they waited until it got louder and louder.
They turned around and ran, it was a giant fairy. They were scared so they ran. The giant fairy started looking, she looked behind the tree and a few flowers. The fairies fell asleep and they didn't notice the big fairy going back home.
In the morning they saw the door. They rushed through the door and collected the rest of the apples.

Sophie Ridsdale (6)

St Luke's Primary School, Brighton

The Fairy Who Wanted To Go To The Pool

One roasting morning, a fairy wanted to go to Fairy Land, so she could go in the pool. She invited her friend to come with her. They set off, but they forgot their roses. On the way they found a magic door to the swimming pool. They were just in the changing room when her friend jumped and she was amazed. She went underwater. Then her friend went down the water slide. There was a cliff to jump off, and they fell off it and landed in a swamp and she used her wings to pull herself out. She came out and flew away. She went back to her palace and she was tired and she was sleeping, so she shut the door and said bye.

Sylvie Eliza King (6)
St Luke's Primary School, Brighton

The Lion And The Haunted House

Once upon a time there was a lion called Jonny. One sunny day he decided to go for a walk so he went to the jungle. As he was walking he saw a dusty wooden door, and he thought about it, so he said to himself, 'I want to go through,' so he did. But when he got through it was a haunted house. He tiptoed along and saw a skeleton walking along. As he turned around a corner, he saw a slender man and some tarantulas were hanging from their webs. When he went to the attic he saw lots of bats. He realised that a witch was watching him, he got his bag and drilled a hole in the wall to escape.

Jesse Hogan (6)
St Luke's Primary School, Brighton

The Talking Sausage

Once upon a time in a six-year-old girl's tummy there lived a sausage. One day he was running in her tummy. He was climbing on the edges trying to escape when he saw a door and went through. On the other side a giant was playing with his giant marble-run. The marble-run was very colourful and the sausage climbed the sides. When the giant came along he threw a marble in the marble-run. The sausage pushed and pushed and after a couple of hours he got the marble to bounce out and he ran through the magic door. He went back home.

Alice Hogan (6)
St Luke's Primary School, Brighton

Rogow's Big Adventure

One Christmas morning, Rogow the robot looked at the tree he planted, when he saw a wooden door in it. He decided to go through it. At the other side there was a jungle with creepy-crawlies that groaned and moaned. Rogow the robot went further into the jungle and heard a rumbling above him. It was a volcano! He ran away from the volcano, and ran all the way back to the magic door and went through it. When he was on the other side he hammered wood to the door, so nobody could come out. When he finished it he had a big lunch.

Maxwell Robinson (6)
St Luke's Primary School, Brighton

Poppy The Kitten

One sunny Monday morning, there lived a kitten called Poppy. She lived with her mum and dad.

One day, in the morning, a door appeared in her bedroom. Poppy decided to go through it. Poppy ended up in Wishing World. She saw lots of gold. Poppy saw a castle, so she went in it. In the castle she saw a crown, but it wasn't only a crown, it was a ghost crown. A ghost came out of the crown and the ghost chased Poppy.

Poppy ran out of the castle and back through the magic door and locked the door forever and ran back home.

Echo Capaldi (6)

St Luke's Primary School, Brighton

The Poo Story

One day, a clean happy poo lived in someone's bottom, he was a very nice poo. He had poo friends too, they had parties all day. He had a poo disco.

One day he found a door with poo particles, he opened the door and he ended up in Poo Land. He saw poo towers, poo roads and poo houses.

One day he saw a nice, giant, dirty poo who shrank the door. He turned happy poops into him. The happy poo saw a poo train, he told the train driver to take him home. The driver was a friend of his. So he went home with his friend.

Jonah Peter Driver (6)
St Luke's Primary School, Brighton

The Ice Cream And The Angry Flower

Once, there was an ice cream and he was walking down the road trying to catch the ice cream van. In the middle of the road there was a door, so he decided to go through it. He found himself in Flower Land. He was having fun with the happy flowers. Suddenly, an angry flower came and turned all of the happy flowers into sad flowers, then they all tried to eat the ice cream. But he had an idea, he spilled ice cream on the angry flowers, then he rushed to the door and carried on chasing the ice cream van.

Noa McQue-Moore (6)

St Luke's Primary School, Brighton

History

One nice morning there was a witch who lived in a creepy castle. One day she was going for a walk and she found a magic door. So the witch went through it. She saw lots of fascinating people. She saw lots of fascinating cars rushing around, she also saw some pirates. The witch started a battle with the pirates for food. She didn't know what to do. Then she saw a shop. She went to the shop then she saw a sword so she took the sword back to the battle, and defeated all the pirates, then she went back home.

Florrie Rees-Francis (6)
St Luke's Primary School, Brighton

Zone Mix 1

Deep in the ocean lived a wolf eel. His best friend was Brittle Star. Suddenly, an undersea storm came! The wolf eel tried to run away but the storm sucked him in. 'Shhh! Ahh!'
He woke up in a different zone of the ocean and he met lots of friends. He figured out which zone he was in. The Sunlight Zone. Suddenly a whale shark swallowed him! But he wasn't lunch yet. He tickled the whale shark and it opened its mouth but he didn't know which way was home! He had to stay the night.

Ivan Qiam (6)
St Luke's Primary School, Brighton

Pokémon Land

Once upon a time there lived a Pokémon called Stargaze and he was a fire type Pokémon.
One sunny day Stargaze was watching TV, suddenly there was a door and he decided to go through. When he got through he was amazed by the land he saw. It was Pokémon Land! He saw Pokémon everywhere he looked. Suddenly, a train came to him. He ran for his life. He jumped onto the train. 'Hey!' said the driver.
He ran off the train and he lived happily ever after.

Gwilym Harris (6)
St Luke's Primary School, Brighton

Untitled

Once, there was a girl called Evie and she was watching TV with her little pet chameleon. Suddenly, they started whizzing around.
They realised they were in magic popping candy! Then everything was still, absolutely still. Evie gasped, there were teachers everywhere using magic!
Suddenly, a horrible witch appeared and chased them! But luckily for them the magic popping candy was there, so they jumped into it and were whizzed home.

Edith May Fisher (6)
St Luke's Primary School, Brighton

The Story Of The Land

One roasting hot morning, a unicorn and leopard were playing in their garden. They went to get a drink and they strolled along to the river.
They remembered that they had left their suncream at home. They ran back and grabbed the suncream, when they saw a door. They jumped in then opened the door and went to a Mountain World. But they turned red because they were spooky mountains. They climbed the mountains, then came back down and went home.

Milly McNicol (6)
St Luke's Primary School, Brighton

Untitled

One rainy day, a little tiger was in his home in the sea. He went for a picnic in the play park. Just then he spotted a door and decided to go through. When he went through it, he was in Same World. In this world everyone looks the same. When he looked around he saw no pets... he *was* the pet. Two children came out of their house and started to snatch the tiger. Luckily, the tiger had his bag. In his bag was a parachute so he parachuted home and locked the door.

Honey Lemmon (6)

St Luke's Primary School, Brighton

The Elf And The Unicorn

Once upon a time there was an elf and a unicorn. They lived in a forest and they liked to play hide-and-seek in the trees.

Suddenly, a glimmer of yellow appeared and when it was gone, a magic door appeared. The elf and the unicorn rushed through...

They found out that they were in Snow Land. Suddenly, a snow monster appeared but the unicorn used its magic to melt it and they walked back to the door, and went back to their forest.

Lydia Stockel (6)

St Luke's Primary School, Brighton

The Teleporting Door

One day a boy was creeping out of his mum's window. From the corner of his eye he saw a shutdown golden door, and decided to go in it. When he was inside, he fell through a door. He slept forever. Finally he woke up and didn't know where he was. He looked around, he saw a spring trap! He was so scared that he crawled through a vent that took him back home.

Yolo Gunnar Woodman (6)

St Luke's Primary School, Brighton

Blob Goes To Mow Land

Once upon a time there was Blob who lived in a slimy rubbish dump.

One morning, Blob was looking for an old rotation bed. He saw a magic door so he went through. It took Blob to Mowland. He heard music, it said, 'Mow mow mow mow!'

There was a creature. It said, 'I'm Mow Mow.' Then a rock slide came.

'Do it!' said Blob. Blob got a sword and sliced the rocks.

Lenny Lovesey (6)
St Luke's Primary School, Brighton

Untitled

On a roasting day, there was a cheeky cat that was called Explorer. He lived in a tree house.
The next morning he went to the pond and he dug a hole in the sand. When he finished he saw a magic door. He was the first cat to be in City World and saw a forest. He went in and a monster found him. He heard a sound and saw him. He found a magic bag and took a rock out, and threw it at the monster.

George Wadsworth (6)
St Luke's Primary School, Brighton

The Adventure Of Alice And Jesse

Once upon a time there was a princess called Alice and a king called Jesse. They had a tiger.
They were bored so they went for a little walk The soldiers came back and asked what had happened to them! Jesse and Alice stepped out of the magic door. They had been in the jungle and had jumped on a tiger. The tiger roared and came to live with Jesse and Alice in the castle.

Ryan Terry Goodier (6)
St Luke's Primary School, Brighton

The TV

One sunny day, Evie lived in a rainbow house with her little sister, Bella. The street was Rochester Street. Suddenly, Evie was chased by the TV and got eaten. It was a shock for Evie because she ended up in a jungle. The TV decided to go so off he went. Evie finally got home with her little sister to watch TV, but it wasn't a normal TV ever again.

Bella Soper (6)
St Luke's Primary School, Brighton

Poo Land

Once there was a boy called Oliver. One day he went to the toilet, then he realised that it was a toilet that went to Poo Land. He decided to flush himself down. When he got to Poo Land, he started to play with the poos. After that he had a nap but there was a poo monster! Quickly he got a poo poison and killed it.

Oliver O'Connell (6)
St Luke's Primary School, Brighton

The Magic TV

One day, Alia was watching TV with her spotty pet chameleon. They were watching 'Harry Potter and the Deathly Hallows' when suddenly Voldemort jumped out of the TV! He chased them into the woods. When they came out, they fought. But Harry Potter came to the rescue! Then Alia went home.

Alia Cheverton (6)

St Luke's Primary School, Brighton

Untitled

One day, a chameleon and a chicken were watching TV. Suddenly the TV flashed. *Whoosh!* They got sucked in. They were in Legoland, on the submarine ride, and they saw a shark trying to break the submarine, but the chameleon used his long tongue to make a ship to go home.

Lucas Taylor (6)

St Luke's Primary School, Brighton

Evie And The Magic Door

Evie was playing on the sandy beach. She saw a big door beside her. She opened the door and went in... When she looked around she saw sweets. She was in Candy Land! Then she saw a witch. Evie ran away. The witch lost her. Evie saw a magic carpet. She went back home.

Lorelai Vincent (6)
St Luke's Primary School, Brighton

Untitled

Roamrooch was in her room watching TV and
eating her yummy breakfast, when she ate a piece
of her food she was teleported into Candyland.
She met a friendly gingerbread man, they came
across a giant chocolate bar. They couldn't get
home, and nearly had a fight.

Macy Mead (6)
St Luke's Primary School, Brighton

Bella And The Tiger

One day, Bella was watching TV with her blonde gerbil. Suddenly, a swirling thing came out of the floor, she stepped into it. When she came out she was in a forest. But a tiger chased her all the way home.

Poppy Ryan (6)
St Luke's Primary School, Brighton

A Mystery

Once upon a time there was a girl called McKenzie and a teacher called Rose. McKenzie was the only kid in the school.

The next day, McKenzie was playing when suddenly a door caught her eye. She went over to the door and saw a little key. She unlocked the door and got sucked in. She opened her eyes and *boom!* there was a flash of light. She screamed, 'Where am I'? She kept on walking until she found a little piece of paper, it said something but she didn't know what it meant. She finally figured out the riddle and kept on walking. She found an invisibility cloak and put it on. She saw a house next to the door, there was an old rusty key, she put the key in the keyhole but the door didn't open. She thought of an idea, kept on walking and wiped the key. It had something written on it. She carried on walking but as she turned left she saw the door and she put the key in it. She got sucked in the door and there was a flash of a light. She was back where she started.

She went inside the class and they lived happily ever after.

Israa Tribak (7)

St Paul's Way Foundation School, London

The Scary Forest

Many moons ago, there lived a brother and a sister called Jennie and James. Jennie was 10 years old and James was 7 years old.

One day, they went to a play park. When they were playing, they saw a magic door. They opened it and it took them to a very scary forest! They were both very scared, but then came a voice and it was... a witch! But it was a nice witch. She said, 'Don't be scared, I won't hurt you, I'm a nice witch.' So Jennie and James said, 'OK.'

But it was a trick! She quickly got James and he shouted, 'Help!' The witch was very cunning and took James away.

Jennie ran after them and said, 'Give back my brother!' The witch wouldn't give him back. Jennie had a bag of stuff to save people with, so she had an idea. She got her fencing armour and went to the witch's tower, then she defeated the witch with great bravery and they lived happily ever after.

Jannah Kolil Uddin (7)
St Paul's Way Foundation School, London

War Underwater

One day, a boy called Finny was in his house, he found the basement and Finny teleported underwater with his sister and dog. Shelby the dog turned into Dogfish, Charlotte (Finny's sister) turned into a Water Girl and Finny turned into Shark Boy. The problem was, they wanted to be themselves not a dogfish or a water girl or a shark boy!

So they met a shark, he knew answers to all the questions in the world. Finny asked, 'How do we go to our home and how do we turn back to humans?' 'The only way to turn back to humans is to breathe above the ocean, and the way to get to your home is to go back the way you came from!'

'Thank you, Mr Shark!'

They turned back to humans and they found the magic door. They opened the door? They went in and then they were home and they all lived happily ever after.

Mohammed Shayaan Abdullah (7)

St Paul's Way Foundation School, London

Cheeco And The Wicked Witch

Once upon a time there lived a girl called McKenzie and her dog Cheeco. They were going to Egypt on a plane but they crashed in a desert in Morocco. Under the plane they saw a key... it spoke to them. It told them where to find the door and a picture of a witch.

A few days later, Cheeco and McKenzie were thirsty and starving, they couldn't find food at all. They saw a dark, creepy house in the distance, the further they went into the house the more their hearts beat. When McKenzie went upstairs, all of the witches came out of their cages, except one, the baby witch. They couldn't fix the problem until they asked the kind baby witch to help. They escaped and lived happily ever after.

Ayah Tribak (7)
St Paul's Way Foundation School, London

Sam, Max And Stan

One Saturday morning, when Sam and Max were playing in the play park, Max sniffed out a strange, shiny door, so Sam and Max opened it. When they went in, they ended up in a world full of sweets! They ate sweets for a day and a half. Suddenly, Sam and Max got chased by a monster called Stan. When Sam and Max were running they found a magic cloak and they transformed into sweets. When Stan wasn't looking, Sam and Max took the cloak off and hid behind some sweets.

When the monster was gone they ran to the magic door. They got back to the play park. Miss Cherry (Sam's teacher) told him to take his dog home then go to school.

Jedidiha Dobamo Aleling (8)
St Paul's Way Foundation School, London

Henry And Pat

Once upon a time in a spooky and dark forest, there lived a boy called Pat and a dog called Henry. They saw a door and the door took them to a spooky adventure.
When they started the spooky adventure, they heard scary noises, it was spooky and dark!
They could never get out the spooky adventure, but they had a plan... use a map.
They saw a monster called Pinky, he tried to eat them but Pat turned giant by eating poison that makes you grow! Pat turned invisible, and he tried to squash Pinky but he was too squishy like jelly.
Henry, Pat and Pinky played with each other and they lived happily ever after.

Blake Liam Michael Power (6)

St Paul's Way Foundation School, London

Astro-Man's Adventure On The Moon

One day, there was an astronaut called Astro-Man who flew his aluminium rocket onto the moon. He explored the moon and noticed a teleport hidden in a crater. He jumped into the teleport and ended up on Pluto.

Astro-Man explored the cold planet Pluto, he turned around and saw that the teleport was guarded by aliens. How weird! Luckily, Astro-Man had found two space rocks and threw them at the aliens. They disappeared, the teleport was free. Astro-Man jumped back into the teleport, ended up on the moon, then flew his rocket back to Planet Earth. He was safe!

Feliks Szyszka (7)
St Paul's Way Foundation School, London

The Spooky Door

Far, far away lived a mum called Rebecca, a boy called Sammy and a girl called Ellie. They lived in Australia and they went to the park. In the park there were rides, people and parents. The ran across the path and saw a tree with a door on it. They opened the door and there was a spooky park, so they joined it. Then they saw that the door had vanished. They panicked and panicked. To solve the problem they found a map and that map led them to a different door, this door led them back to the play park.
They finally got home and had a good night's sleep.

Ava Miah (7)
St Paul's Way Foundation School, London

The Magical Door

Many moons ago, there was a play park. In this play park there was a party. It was Rose's birthday. Rose saw a magic door on one of the trees! She screamed, 'Wow!' Rose went inside the magic door and it took her to a spooky forest. It was all dark and gloomy. She was petrified of a witch called Pinha. Pinha cast a spell on the magic door and *poof*, it was gone!

Luckily, Rose found a map. 'This map will show the way to the magic door!' said Rose.

Zoharin Choudhury Tabassum (7)

St Paul's Way Foundation School, London

Untitled

Many moons ago in a spooky forest there was a boy called Harry and a dog called Max. They both played in the spooky forest and saw a magic door. They went on a spooky adventure!
They saw skeletons and zombies. Max became angry, then he barged through the skeletons. Harry used the invisibility cloak. Max did a spinning tornado. The skeletons and the zombies were defeated. They both went home and lived happily ever after.

Jibrael Abdur-Rahman (7)

St Paul's Way Foundation School, London

The Bad Witch

One sunny day, I saw a big door in a tree. I opened the door and went through. I had an adventure. My mum and grandma came as well. I went to the park. But there was a witch. She was bad. Me and my mum made the witch good because the witch was in my family. We made her good by feeding her potions, then we had a party because she was very nice.

Olivia Karamac (6)
St Paul's Way Foundation School, London

The Magic Door

I was in Fairy Land. But oh no! I did not have wings. I saw a shop that sold fairy wings, so I went inside and a boy sold them to me. I told him my story, then we went to have a picnic in the park. The boy said 'Hi, my name is Sam.'

'My name is Florence.'

'Hi Florence, I think we should have a picnic here!'

'Good idea Sam.'

'So what we have got is this yoghurt? Grapes and more fruit, but wait a minute, what's that? It's a wizard!'

'What?'

'I am a nice wizard, I won't do any harm to you.'

'We have paté and lots of pizza.'

'But the witch is still alive!'

'No, not the witch! Run!'

'Come on it's time to go to bed.'

So I went back through the door and back home.

Florence Osman (6)

St Swithun Wells Catholic Primary School, Chandlers Ford

The Magic Door

I was in a spooky forest with broken trees and lanterns everywhere and I was wearing a spooky spider dress. 'What a spooky place this is!' Then I saw a haunted house and there was a ghost behind a broken tree! I did not see it because I was in the house. Then when I was opening the door, the ghost was behind it. I could not get out. Then the ghost left and I opened the door and went to explore.
When I came back the ghost was in front of the door and he ate it! We had to build it again, it took a long time. We needed lots of wood and lots of sticks. The ghost was sorry so I forgave him and I took him home. Then we had a picnic.

Michelle Appiah (6)
St Swithun Wells Catholic Primary School, Chandlers Ford

The Party

I saw a party and I was a fairy. Everyone was a fairy. Even my dog was a fairy. I was the birthday girl.
But then the presents were stolen by a fairy witch. I found the presents and gave them back. The fairy witch was angry. We finished the party and I went home with party bags. The witch was so angry she vanished into the woods.

Grace Amelia Rayner (6)

St Swithun Wells Catholic Primary School, Chandlers Ford

What Happened In The Forest?

One sunny day I was walking my dog when I noticed a magic door hidden in a tree. It took me to a spooky forest. I wondered where I was, but just then I noticed something... no, someone! A boy walked out of a bush! When he saw me he was startled. When he was just about to jump back into a tree, I said, 'Wait, I want to be your friend!' With that simple sentence, he ran towards me. He said his name was Alfie. We decided to go on an adventure.

We walked and walked until we came to a spooky castle. It had nearly crumbled to bits but still stood. We went inside to explore, but then Alfie stepped on a loose floorboard... well, that's what we thought it was but it was actually a trapdoor that led to a dungeon. A cage door instantly shut behind him. I was shocked. Then when I looked down an ugly witch came into view. She was so pleased that she had finally caught a person not an animal. When I looked down I saw some animals, such as unicorns, golden squirrels, silver ants, butterflies and many more.

The witch (whose name was Creepy) didn't see me. Creepy caught things to eat and make spells with. She was planning to use Alfie's blood in a spell to make her strong. She was going to use the unicorns' horns for it as well and several other things. I suddenly noticed that I was holding a map of secret passages all around the castle. I was so amazed by it that I did not notice the witch peering through the trapdoor. I quickly got out of view and then I went through one of the secret passages. I was nearly at the dungeon. I opened the cage with a key I found and let all the animals go free. Then we ran as fast as lightning to the door in the tree!

Lola Sophia Uppal Watkinson (7)
Whitehall Park School, Islington

The Stolen Crown

Once, there was a girl called Emma. She was walking her dog, Twitch, when Emma noticed a magic door on a tree. It took her and Twitch to a campsite. There was a teacher called Miss Lime. She was camping. The sun was setting so they went to bed.

A fairy woke Twitch up, so Twitch woke up Emma. It turns out the fairy was called Clara. She took them into space, to the moon. There was a party on the moon but the fairy queen was sad. Emma asked Clara what was wrong with the fairy queen. Clara said that she had lost her crown. So Emma promised Clara they wouldn't come back until they had found the fairy queen's crown. Clara gave both of them wings.

They flew from planet to planet, the last was Saturn, the crown was in its rings. They got it and flew back to the moon. They got back to the moon and Twitch sniffed the thieves out. It was a monster at the very bottom of the moon. Twitch asked the monster why he had been stealing, so he said that he was lonely and he thought it would make him happy.

Twitch said, 'If you come and say sorry we will be your friends!' So they went back to the top of the moon.

The monster said sorry and they had a party. Then Clara said that it was nearly morning, so she took them back to the campsite.

In the morning they told Miss Lime what had happened and she said that it was a dream, but when they looked under their pillows they saw a party bag and some moon rocks.

Rosie Simmons (6)
Whitehall Park School, Islington

A Spooky Forest

One sunny day I was walking my dog when I noticed a magic door hidden in a tree. I opened the door, it took me to a spooky forest. I was walking my dog through the spooky forest and suddenly I bumped into a witch. The witch said, 'Drink this potion!'

'I don't want to drink it!' I said.

The witch said, 'OK, but you have to get me some magic keys!'

I said, 'OK.' I asked, 'What does the dog have to do?'

The witch said, 'He doesn't have to do anything.'

So I went to find the two magic keys. The witch let us out of the spooky forest. On the way to find the magic keys we saw camels and we travelled to a desert. In the desert we found a massive house. The magic key had to be in there so I went in with the camels. We found the first magic key. We had a party, then I got back on the camels and carried on.

We remembered that the second magic key was in the sea so we went to get some suits to get in the water. We also got a sloth. Then we went in the water, it took a long time because a sloth is slow.

We finally got there. Then I got off the sloth and then I dived in the water to get the second magic key, then I just remembered that the witch gave me a potion to get back. I drank it and then I got back to the spooky forest. Then I said to the witch, 'I have got the magic keys.'
The witch said, 'Thank you, you can go now and never come back!'

Clemy Katz (6)
Whitehall Park School, Islington

The Magic Door

One sunny day I was walking my dog, when I noticed a magic door hidden in a tree. I opened the door and it took me to a spooky forest on an island. As soon as I got in the door I got stuck in a house. I searched for days looking for a way out. I searched again and again, until one day I found the beach. But I noticed a witch guarding a lifeboat.

The next morning I woke up very early so I could check if the witch was there. She was waiting, so I threw a rock at her, and as quick as a flash ran to the boat, but the witch put a spell on the sand! I fell down a hole that appeared under me. It took me to the forest again! I heard a noise when I landed on the grassy area. I thought it was laughing, so I followed the noise. But it led me to the door. I remembered I knew the way to the beach from here, so I set off. I did the same thing as before, but I went around the trap. I took a lot of food and fresh water. I taught my dog how to row and that made it much easier, and I finally found land and I found my mum.

Gabriel Baden (7)
Whitehall Park School, Islington

The Search!

One sunny day, I was walking my dog when I noticed a magic door hidden in a tree. I opened the door and it took me to a play park! The play park was full of children. I saw my friends and they said, 'There is a problem to be solved,' so we set off. We got there quickly by the bus. Finally we got there.

We saw that the king and queen were very, very sad. 'What is wrong?' I said.

'We have lost our powers,' the king said sadly. They'd searched and searched but they couldn't find their powers.

The queen said, 'Will we ever find our powers?'

Suddenly Emma saw a sparkle of light. We all went to it, it was the king and queen's powers! They were so happy and amazed.

I woke up and got dressed and went to school.

Anouk Lola Archet-Elsley (6)

Whitehall Park School, Islington

The Mermaids And The Sea Monster

One sunny day I was walking my dog when I noticed a magic door hidden behind a tree, I opened the door and it took me under the sea. When I was under the sea I saw an underwater castle. Lots of mermaids were having a big party because it was the queen mermaid's birthday. Suddenly, a big slimy sea monster came and all the mermaids swam away. They were very scared. Then another sea monster came and it was the mermaid's sea monster friend. The friendly monster fought off the evil monster.

After that they had a big party and they had doughnuts with sprinkles on top and fairy cupcakes. Then they did lots of dancing and played games.

Finally, I went back home to have supper and lived happily ever after.

Helen Kim Wood (7)
Whitehall Park School, Islington

The Three Witches, The Three Monsters And The Three Wizards

Once upon a time lived three little witches, one of them was called Lola and she was the biggest. The second biggest was called Alice and the smallest witch was called Matilda.

One day, the three witches realised that three monsters lived on their land. So they got very angry. They made a spell that can kill monsters. There also lived three wizards that gave the monsters life. The witches got even angrier so they made a spell that would definitely kill the three monsters. The wizards gave the three monsters life again, but they could not do any more magic. After three years the three witches became old and died.

Alisa Makarova (6)
Whitehall Park School, Islington

Emma, Ben And The Spider

One sunny day, Emma and Ben were walking their dog when they noticed a magic door hidden in a tree. It took them to a tunnel. They saw something at the end of it. Suddenly, they were grabbed by their legs. Then they were on a spider's web, so they said to the spider that made it, 'We're not going to hurt your babies!'
So he let them go and they had spaghetti for dinner.

Izzy Potton
Whitehall Park School, Islington

Untitled

A teacher was walking along the path with her dog when she found a magic door. She wondered what it could be. She opened it and saw witches, ghosts and monsters. She thought she was stuck there forever. 'Wait a minute!' she cried. 'I can go the way I came!' She got back to Whitehall Park School again.

Genevieve Outten (6)

Whitehall Park School, Islington

First published in Great Britain in 2018 by:

Young Writers
Remus House
Coltsfoot Drive
Peterborough
PE2 9BF
Telephone: 01733 890066
Website: www.youngwriters.co.uk

Young Writers Information

We hope you have enjoyed reading this book and that you will continue to in the coming years.

If you're a young writer who enjoys reading and creative writing, or the parent of an enthusiastic poet or story writer, do visit our website **www.youngwriters.co.uk**. Here you will find free competitions, workshops and games, as well as recommended reads, a poetry glossary and our blog.

If you would like to order further copies of this book, or any of our other titles give us a call or visit **www.youngwriters.co.uk**.

Young Writers
Remus House
Coltsfoot Drive
Peterborough
PE2 9BF

(01733) 890066
info@youngwriters.co.uk